Best Friends For Life

Trollz™

Best Friends For Life

Adapted by Jennifer Miller

SCHOLASTIC INC.

New York   Toronto   London   Auckland   Sydney
Mexico City   New Delhi   Hong Kong   Buenos Aires

Designed by Pamela Darcy

ISBN 0-439-73387-1

12 11 10 9 8 7 6 5 4 3 2 1   5 6 7 8 9/0

Printed in the U.S.A.
First printing, October 2005

Best Friends For Life

The late summer sun glistened over Trollzopolis, illuminating the rainbow of bright colors that encompassed the city's contemporary skyline. The enormous Trollzopolis mega-mall loomed large, glittering in the distance. Its trendy shops and trollicious food court made it a destination for teen trollz from all over the city.

Topaz, Sapphire, Onyx, and Ruby parked their state-of-the-art hover skoots on the smoldering asphalt of the mall's parking lot and dismounted in unison.

"On time — no minutes to spare," Sapphire announced, checking her watch.

The girls whipped off their helmets — their huge hairdos popped out perfectly.

"Time for a troll stroll," Ruby announced, snapping her fingers and shaking her flaming red hair. The group paraded forward in step.

Inside, Amethyst sipped a soft drink and awaited the arrival of her friends. It was the last week of summer before the new school year. She hadn't seen her friends since she left to visit her grandmother at the beginning of the summer.

"Amethyst!" they cried in unison as they spotted her across the food court. Amethyst leaped up from her chair to hug Topaz and Sapphire while Onyx and Ruby sauntered over.

"Watch the hair," Ruby cautioned as she eased into a careful hug.

"Hi, Onyx," Amethyst said, smiling.

"Squeal with delight and I'll puke." Onyx frowned as she leaned in to give Amethyst a trollnormous hug.

"I'm so happy to see you guys!" Amethyst exclaimed. "Last night I had this weird dream that I didn't fit in with you anymore."

Sapphire shook her blue mop of hair. "That's crazy," she said.

"Yeah," Ruby chimed in. "Nobody busts up the crew."

"I mean, how can we be Best Friends For Life if we're not best friends *now*, right?" added Topaz. Sometimes her unique brand of logic made the ultimate sense.

Just then, Ruby spotted a cute boy troll. "Cute boy at three o'clock," she whispered.

"But it's only ten-thirty," Topaz chimed in, confused.

"No, over *there*," Ruby said, pointing.

The group turned and watched as the boy self-consciously strode by. They stopped talking and gazed at him dreamily.

"Hottie!" exclaimed Ruby.

"Lost soul," Onyx surmised.

"Digital sneakers," Topaz noticed.

Amethyst suddenly felt out of touch. "Um . . . he looks like he might be understanding and fun to study with?" she chimed in.

Her friends stared at her as if she'd just sprouted a third arm.

"Somebody is *seriously* out of practice," Sapphire noted with concern.

"Sorry, guys," Amethyst said. "I've been kind of distracted lately." She looked away, feeling her cheeks grow as pink as the hair on her head.

"Why?" Ruby asked. She noticed that Amethyst was blushing.

Amethyst was itching to tell. She felt like she would just burst if she kept it to herself another second.

Her friends' eyes widened and they all leaned in at once. "Spill!" they insisted.

"I wanted to tell you all at the same time," Amethyst said in a whisper. She hopped down from her chair and lifted up her blouse just a bit, revealing a glowing gemstone in her belly button. It glimmered under the food court's fluorescent lights. "My gem got its glow!" she squealed.

"Left home a trollkin, came back a troll," Onyx said with a laugh, her black eyes twinkling.

Amethyst was the last of her friends to get her glow. Now she could finally cast spells like the rest of them! With everyone in on the spells, they were going to have a fun school year. Her face hurt from grinning.

"It's about time you joined us," Ruby pronounced. "So show us a spell."

Amethyst hesitated. Her grandmother had warned her not to waste spells. "I don't know . . . spell beads are expensive," she said. "Plus I only have a few spell beads that my grandmother gave me in case of an emergency."

Ruby lifted her wrist to reveal a charm bracelet with a dozen small amber spell beads on it. She popped off two at once and tossed one to Amethyst.

"Here!" she said. "I've got drawers full of 'em." This was no surprise to her friends. The crew all knew that Ruby was just a tad spoiled.

"Me first, though," Ruby said as she held up the amber bead and studied it. "Oh, cool! We both got transformation spells!"

Just then, a middle-aged troll lady trudged by in drab clothes and her hair in rollers.

"She could use some help," Ruby observed. She held up the bead and chanted:

**"Drab and dreary, walking by,
Look pretty as a butterfly!"**

In an instant, the troll lady transformed into a colorful, troll-sized butterfly. Unaware of her transformation, she continued along, hovering with her new wings flapping.

Onyx shook her head of poofy purple hair. "A new hairdo would've been fine, Rube." Onyx could always be counted on to get right to the point.

"It'll wear off," Ruby said. "Eventually."

Onyx put her arm around Amethyst. "Can you help us out here, rookie?" she pleaded.

Amethyst held up her spell bead, nervous but determined. It was her first spell. Would it even work? She hesitated. "I can't," she said quietly.

"You can do it!" Sapphire said firmly, adjusting her glasses and staring at the bead with intensity. Then she added, under her breath, "Though transformation spells can be tricky. You *could* just make things worse."

There was no getting out of it. Amethyst took a deep breath and her lavender eyes shone as she concentrated on the spell bead.

**"Trapped in a body not your own,
Release your spirit to the shape you've known."**

The group gaped in delight as the troll lady transformed back into herself, although she now wore a styling new outfit and a colorful hairdo.

"Gelled to the max!" Sapphire said, beaming at Amethyst.

Onyx was seriously impressed. "You're a natural at this magic stuff, troll," she said.

"Yeah," Topaz added. "We could have a new spells champ."

Ruby crossed her arms dramatically as her face flushed with jealousy. "We *could* just have beginner's luck!" she snapped. "I guess I need to go where my magic is appreciated!" She turned abruptly and stormed off.

Sapphire sighed. "Time to calm down the drama queen," she said. "C'mon, Topaz. Let's go."

"What did I do?" Amethyst asked, confused.

"Nothing," Onyx assured her. "Ruby's just not used to you outdoing her. It'll be fine. I've gotta run. Sadly, I'm late for my dentist and his dark room of pain. But c'mon over later and we'll talk, OK?"

Amethyst stood alone, crushed. Above all, she wanted her friends to be a trollegiance. And the first day back she'd made Ruby mad by just being herself. Her nightmare had come true! She no longer fit in with her friends, and now she would have to start high school as a loner with no one to talk to. Had she really changed that much?

2

Amethyst rifled through the rubble in her closet until she finally found her cherished memory book. As she settled on her bed, her troll Chihuahua, Wa-wa, hopped up beside her. "Hi, Wa-wa," she said, gently petting his soft fur. She placed the memory book on her lap. "Memory book, on!" she said as she opened the book to reveal a flat-panel computer screen. The book flickered on at her voice command. A close-up moving picture of her at ten or eleven years old, sticking her tongue out at the camera, appeared as the screen saver. *Gonna have to update that*, she thought to herself, realizing she hadn't looked at the book in awhile. As she scrolled through the memory book, various video recordings from the past appeared.

The memory book's screen cut to a recording from several years earlier. The five best friends danced hand in hand around a campfire, wearing their pajamas and looking goofy. Everyone except Ruby wore a daisy chain in her hair. Laughing, Amethyst tried to put a daisy chain in Ruby's hair. "Watch the hair," Ruby snapped, waving her off.

Some things never change, Amethyst thought as she scrolled through the book to another memory.

She came across an image of eight-year-old Sapphire. "Hey, I know!" Sapphire was telling her friends. "Let's play Girl Power Tower."

"Amethyst, you and Onyx on the bottom," Ruby commanded.

"We always get the bottom," Onyx grumbled as they piled into a human pyramid and crashed to the ground in a heap, laughing as they tumbled.

"Mystic Waterfall!" Amethyst said to the memory book. Now the screen displayed an image of Ruby, Amethyst, Sapphire, Topaz, and Onyx as they stood on the edge of a pool at the base of a beautiful waterfall. The girls glanced at one another and then tensed to make a jump.

"All right, here we go!" Ruby said. "Wait a sec! Amethyst, we need you to run the camera."

Disappointed, Amethyst stepped back from the group and moved toward the camera, watching as her friends leaped hand in hand into the water.

"Girl Power!" the four girls screamed with delight.

Amethyst closed the memory book and tossed it aside. She hugged Wa-wa. "Now I get why I don't fit in anymore, Wa-wa." She sighed. "I never used to do anything but follow them around and do what they wanted. But I can't be that way anymore! I mean, I've changed. Haven't I?"

Wa-wa barked playfully in response and then licked her hand, but it wasn't much of an answer.

* * * *

The next day at the mall, Amethyst watched as Topaz tried on a particularly funky outfit. Over the summer, Topaz's off-the-wall personality had translated into an off-the-wall ensemble that involved several intensely clashing colors and patterns. Amethyst tried to be positive, but wound up trying too hard.

"So, whaddya think?" Topaz asked eagerly as she did a little twirl in the bizarre outfit.

"It's, um, great," she said, smiling brightly. "The shirt and the pants are sort of like uncoordinated coordinates!"

Topaz picked up on Amethyst's overeager response. She slinked back into the dressing room, offended.

Later that same day, Amethyst and Sapphire were hanging out in Sapphire's bedroom. Sapphire was prouder of her smarts than anything else, and her bedroom was no different. The walls were lined with books, galaxy mobiles hung from the ceiling, and computer equipment was piled neatly in every nook and cranny. Sapphire proudly held up a small blue envelope and showed it to Amethyst.

"What's that?" Amethyst asked.

"It's only my acceptance into the most impossible-to-get-into trollzology course in the school," Sapphire boasted.

"Wow! That's really cool, Sapphire," Amethyst said as she gave her friend a hug.

But then Sapphire noticed that Amethyst had an identical envelope sticking out of her skirt belt.

"You got in, too?" she asked, deflated.

Amethyst shrugged. "Yeah, but that's great, right?" she asked her friend. "I mean, we can study together and everything!"

"Uh, yeah," Sapphire responded. "Sure!"

But she didn't look convinced.

The next day, Amethyst and Onyx hung out in Onyx's bedroom. Her bedroom perfectly matched her personality. She wore and said things nobody else would dare to, and her room gave off the same vibe. It was primarily black and gray, but it was anything but dull. Posters for bands Amethyst had never heard of lined the walls, and Onyx sat on her bed, which featured a looming headboard carved out of black wood in twisting detail and speckled with cobwebs.

"Onyx, I don't know what to do!" Amethyst lamented. "These past few days, I can't seem to do anything right. I've been trying to be just like I was before I got my glow, but it seems like all of my friends hate me now. I'm totally frizzed out!"

"And here I thought you'd come back from your grandmother's so grown up and cool," Onyx said, smiling.

"You did?" Amethyst asked in surprise.

"Sure!" Onyx replied. "And I'll bet Topaz and Sapphire think so, too. You've got your glow now. You're going to be better at some things than Ruby. She doesn't hate you. She's just feeling a teensy-weensy little bit threatened."

"Do you really think so?" Amethyst asked. Onyx's advice was always solid, but Ameythst couldn't help but think it sounded too good to be true.

"I know so," Onyx replied with a wise nod of her head.

"But I don't want Ruby to be mad at me," Amethyst said. "How do I fix it?"

"I'd just let it go," Onyx suggested with a shrug. "But if you really want to talk to her, she's probably at Fizzy's."

3

Fizzy's Amber Caves Café was the ultimate hangout for teen trollz, despite the fact that the hangout's cranky owner, Fizzy, gave all of the kids a hard time.

"Hey, kid!" Fizzy was yelling as Amethyst entered the café. "You gonna order something or are you just gonna sit there like a bump on a log?"

Fizzy had been addressing Flint, an aspiring poet/singer/songwriter who was often off in his own world, conjuring up poems or songs.

Flint felt a sudden flash of inspiration. "Bump on a log . . . knot on the bark . . . howl like a dog . . . hunt like a snark! Now *that's* poetry," he declared, scribbling excitedly in his notebook. Fizzy frowned, looking confused. Then he hobbled off, grumbling as he went.

Amethyst walked over to him. "Um, hi, Flint," she

said shyly. "You might not remember me from last year, but I'm Amethyst. Have you seen Ruby today?"

Still scribbling, Flint answered without looking up. "I've been so deep in my own head, I have not even seen, like, the sun."

"Oh," Amethyst said, dejected. "Well, thanks."

As she turned to go, Flint finally looked up. He saw her for the first time since the previous school year. "Amethyst?" he asked. He suddenly seemed impressed with her new, glowing vibe.

She turned around. "Yes?"

"I'm a bump on a log," he said, grinning.

Just then, Flint's friend, Rock, the top athlete at school, appeared. Rock was a nice guy but not the sharpest tool in the shed.

"Yo! Flint, man!" Rock announced as he sauntered clumsily over to Flint's table. His muscles were so big they seemed to interfere with his ability to walk. "Guess who just bench-pressed 320, four reps of ten? Personal best!" As Rock made his trolliferous announcement, he noticed Amethyst standing next to Flint. "Whoa! We should know each other," he said, gaping openly at Amethyst.

"We do, Rock," she said bluntly. "I'm Amethyst."

Rock seemed puzzled. "I already know a girl named Amethyst."

"Yeah, it's me." Amethyst sighed, exasperated.

Rock was taken aback. "Whoa!" he gasped. "Coincidence." He still didn't quite get it.

Just then, Ruby and Topaz approached the coffeehouse. "Don't you get it?" Ruby snapped. "Think! Amethyst was totally disrespecting you!"

"See, I thought she was just disagreeing with my fashion choices, not belittling my taste and color sense," Topaz mused.

Ruby stopped and gave her a hard look.

"Oh! Now I get it!" Topaz exclaimed, suddenly angry.

Inside the coffeehouse, Ruby was stopped short by what she saw. An expression of horror spread across her face as she spotted Amethyst standing awkwardly between Flint, who was reading his new poem, and Rock, who was flexing his muscles. How could Amethyst do this to her? Rock was *her* boyfriend. Of course, he didn't know that yet, but still. Ruby was outraged.

Amethyst smiled when she saw Ruby, happy to be saved from the less than stellar conversation she was being forced to endure. "Ruby! Am I glad to see you!" She smiled brightly.

"Yeah, I'll bet!" Ruby snapped. "Traitor!"

"No, this is Amethyst," said Rock. He was now more confused than ever.

"Look, Ruby," Amethyst said. "I'm sorry about before. I just want to be in the crew again."

"Right! So that's why you steal my boyfriend?" Ruby demanded.

"Who's that?" Rock interjected.

"You!" exclaimed Ruby.

"Really?" asked Rock, pleased with this new development.

Amethyst started, "But I didn't try to steal your —"

"Cry me a river, build me a bridge," Ruby cut Amethyst off. "And get over it! As far as I'm concerned, you're outta the crew!"

Amethyst stared at Ruby in disbelief. "What?" she murmured softly. Her cheeks grew hot and her vision went blurry as tears suddenly welled up in her eyes. She turned and ran out of the coffeehouse, crying. Ruby smiled triumphantly, but Topaz, Flint, and Rock were taken aback.

"Whoa. That was harsh," Rock said as he surveyed the situation.

"You're taking *her* side?!" Ruby shouted, aghast. "That's it! We're through!" Ruby turned and stormed out.

"Whoa," Rock stammered. "Did we just break up?"

"You'll still have your memories," Topaz sighed, following Ruby out the door.

"Memories of what?" Rock wondered as he scratched his head.

4

Amethyst sat at the kitchen table while her mother baked cookies. She could smell the trollicious scent of melting chocolate chips, but even that wasn't enough to cheer her up. "But, Mom, I didn't do anything," she protested sadly.

Her mother pulled a tray of cookies out of the oven. "I understand, dear. Sometimes friends just grow apart."

But Amethyst didn't *want* to grow apart. She wanted to be back with the crew — her Best Friends For Life. This was totally unfair. Her mother set the tray on a cooling rack right in front of Amethyst.

"Do those have trollnuts?" Amethyst asked excitedly, reaching for a cookie. Her mother swatted her hand away. "Hands off until they're cool," she scolded. "And be patient with your friends."

Amethyst knew her mother was right. She couldn't pretend to be someone else, so she would have to give her friends some time to get used to the new her. But in the meantime, she was lonely.

Across town at Trollze's Salon, the hippest hair salon in the mall, Ruby and Topaz were angling for chairs under the tall, cylindrical dryers. Ruby, her hair damp, hurried to the center dryer. Topaz followed, taking the dryer to Ruby's right.

"This is the best boy-troll viewing spot in the mall," Ruby declared as she eased into her seat.

"You mean you can, like, dry your hair and watch boys at the same time?" Topaz marveled. "Complex!"

The hair-dryer tubes descended, sucking the girls' hair upward as they closed their eyes and smiled, relaxed and happy.

As soon as they opened their eyes, Ruby pointed out a boy across the mall. "What'd I say?" she said, elbowing Topaz. "Cute senior at nine o'clock!" She then gestured to the dryer on her left. "Amethyst, look! He's just perfect for . . ." She stopped mid-sentence, suddenly aware of her faux pas. Both girls looked at the empty seat to Ruby's left — the seat where Amethyst always sat.

Topaz frowned and looked at Ruby. "It makes sense that you miss her," she said.

"Who says I miss her?" Ruby protested, but it was obvious to Topaz. Something had to be done to restore the crew to its former glory.

* * ⁂ *

Later that day at Fizzy's, Topaz conferred with Sapphire and Onyx. As Topaz and Onyx sipped their extra-large iced mochas, Sapphire paced between the two like an expert trial lawyer, attempting to use her skills of deduction to come up with a solution.

"*You* know that Amethyst wants to be back in the crew," she said, turning to Onyx, who nodded in agreement. "And *you* know that Ruby wants Amethyst back in the crew," she said, turning to Topaz, who also nodded. "Yet we all know that it will never happen because Ruby is too proud to admit that she's wrong." Sapphire raised her finger in the air, preparing to conclude dramatically. "Which means . . ." She suddenly stopped, a frown painted across her face. "Which means we can't just fix it and we all just have to stop being friends." It was not quite the triumphant ending she'd hoped for. She swooped down into the booth, defeated.

Onyx, who had her head buried in her hands in frustration, suddenly spoke. "No, Saph," she said. She looked as though a lightbulb had just lit up in her head. "It means we have to do something special, something risky."

Sapphire perked up. "Magic?" she gasped.

As the trio plotted at the coffeehouse, Ruby paused her skoot down the street from Amethyst's house. She held a crumpled piece of paper in her hand, upon which she'd scribbled an apology. Looking down at it, she forced a rehearsal of what she might say to her former friend. "Uh, gee, Am. Just found myself skooting through your neighborhood and thought I'd say hi." She closed her eyes, gritted her teeth, and threw the paper to the ground. "No! I just can't apologize!" Suddenly, the ringing of her spell phone distracted her. "Topaz?" she said into the phone. "What's trollin'?"

On the other end, Topaz feigned nonchalance. "Oh, nothing special," she said, forgetting what she was supposed to say. Onyx nudged her, prompting her on. "Oh, right! Um, Onyx and Sapphire found out about a party at the old clearing. You know, where we used to have sleepovers?"

Ruby was psyched. "A party?!" she asked.

"Yeah," Topaz said. Then, for emphasis, she added, "They said there are gonna be *senior* boys!"

"I'm there!" Ruby declared, stepping back onto her skoot and hurrying home to prepare for the big night ahead.

Topaz smiled as she hung up the phone. Her performance had been Trolloscar-worthy, but their work wasn't even close to done.

Amethyst was sitting on her bed, her arm around Wa-wa and her spell phone cradled under her chin. She listened with intense interest, hoping above all hopes that she'd be invited back into the crew. "What *about* Ruby?" she asked.

Putting on another four-trollztar performance, Topaz explained that Ruby wanted to apologize but was just too embarrassed. Topaz asked Amethyst if she would meet Ruby in the old clearing, so that Ruby could apologize privately. Amethyst agreed. So far the girls' brilliant plan was working!

5

Amethyst closed her spell phone and held it to her chest, elated. The sun had already started to set, and she wasted no time hurrying toward the forest clearing.

As Ruby made her way through the forest to the same clearing, she took out her compact mirror and patted her perfect hair. *Senior boys*, she thought. *They will not be able to resist the hair.*

Amethyst stepped into the clearing, shuddered, and looked around. It was eerie, and there was no sign of Ruby anywhere. "Rubes?" she called out, confused.

At the opposite side of the clearing, Ruby arrived. She looked up from her mirror, displeased. "Either I'm lost or someone needs some serious lessons in throwing a party."

Just outside of the clearing, Sapphire held up a spell

bead as Topaz looked on nervously. Onyx turned from the clearing and commanded, "Now!"

Sapphire held the bead close to her eyes, chanting:

**"Sprig of fir and leaf of clover,
Turn our Topaz into an ogre."**

With that, she tossed the spell bead. It landed at Topaz's feet and exploded. Onyx and Sapphire each raised a forearm to protect their eyes. As the smoke cleared, they watched in amazement as Topaz grew monstrous.

"Gelled," Onyx said, noting the spell's success.

Topaz was at least twice her normal size, and her arms had thickened into the muscular mass of a menacing ogre. Yet she still had a large shock of blond troll hair on top of her head. "How do I look?" she asked in a low, growly voice.

"Perfect," Sapphire stated. "Now let's go scare them back together."

As Ruby entered the small clearing, she spotted Amethyst easing in from the other side. "Amethyst?!" she said in disbelief.

Amethyst smiled and hurried toward her. "Ruby! They said you'd come."

Ruby backed up, crossing her arms defiantly. "Who said I'd come?"

"Just Topaz, I guess," Amethyst said, puzzled. "She said you wanted to apologize for kicking me out of the crew."

"Apologize?!" Ruby exclaimed. "If you think for one minute I intend to . . ."

Ruby was abruptly cut short as Ogre Topaz let out a thunderous roar. Both Amethyst and Ruby stopped in their tracks. "Wh-what was that?" Amethyst whispered.

"Uh, n-nothing," Ruby stammered back. She tried to sound cool, but her knees were shaking. They were both terrified.

Outside of the clearing, Topaz looked for some direction. "What now?" she whispered desperately to her friends.

"I don't know. Grab one of them," Onyx suggested.

As Amethyst and Ruby stood shaking, the now seven-foot-tall Topaz ambled into the clearing, snatched up Amethyst, and slung her over her shoulder. Amethyst pounded her fists on Topaz's back. "Let me go! Let me go!" she screamed.

"Hey!" Topaz groaned. "Easy, Am. That hurts," said Topaz.

Amethyst was screaming so loud she didn't hear Topaz use her name.

Ruby looked frantically around the clearing for something to stop the ogre. "Don't worry, Am! I'm coming!" she shouted.

Topaz rumbled past Onyx and Sapphire and turned so Amethyst couldn't see them. "Now what?" she pleaded.

"Let me go!" Amethyst screamed as she continued to hammer Topaz's back.

Onyx and Sapphire looked at each other and shrugged.

"Um, pretend you're going to eat her!" Sapphire suggested brightly.

Topaz looked down at Amethyst's legs, not quite sure how an ogre would go about eating a troll. Finally, she lifted Amethyst up by her squirming feet and opened her mouth as if she were about to take a big bite.

"Hang on, Am!" Ruby shouted as she charged at Topaz, knocking her forward with a large stick.

"Aaaaa!" Ruby roared as Topaz and Amethyst landed on the ground with a large thud.

Amethyst ran into the waiting arms of Onyx and Sapphire.

"Don't worry, Am," they reassured her. "We're here!"

"And it's not really an ogre — it's Topaz," Sapphire added.

Amethyst was perplexed. "Topaz?" she asked.

In the meantime, Ruby was still facing off with Ogre Topaz. "I'll teach you to try to hurt my friend," she snarled as she brandished the stick like a gladiator.

"Um, guys . . . nobody said anything about big sticks," Topaz shouted to her friends with concern.

"Ruby!" Amethyst yelled. "It's Topaz!"

"Topaz?" Ruby asked with astonishment.

"Well, duh!" Topaz chortled. "I mean, what ogre would bother to wear raw silk with linen?"

"So Amethyst was never in trouble?" Ruby asked, dropping the stick.

"Onyx said you needed something dramatic to remind you how much she means to you," Sapphire answered.

"Well, I said worse than that," Onyx chimed in. "But you get the idea."

Amethyst smiled at Ruby. "Thanks for rescuing me from Topaz," she said.

"Don't get too pleased with yourself," Ruby replied. "I would have done it for anybody."

"Anybody?" Amethyst raised an eyebrow.

Ruby looked for the right words. "Well, anybody I'd miss if she were out of our crew."

Amethyst's smile grew wider. "And it doesn't matter that I changed over the summer?" she asked.

"You mean 'cause you started being yourself and not letting us push you around so much?" Ruby asked in her best tough voice.

"Yeah, I guess," Amethyst said quietly.

Ruby smiled. "I was getting tired of that old Amethyst, anyway."

"Friends again?" Sapphire asked.

"Not just friends," Ruby declared. "BFFL!"

The five shared a big group hug. "Best Friends For Life!" they shouted together.

"Wait a second," said Topaz. "Who's gonna change me back?" She stared down at her ogre body with a grimace.

* * * *

After Topaz had been transformed back into her styling troll self, everyone skooted back to Amethyst's house. Amethyst stood at the door and said good night to her four best friends.

"Don't go out after we leave," Onyx teased. "You might run into an ogre."

Amethyst laughed. "How *is* Topaz?" she asked, peering her head out the door.

Topaz's clothes were rumpled and frayed. She lowered her head and spit a couple of times, a disgusted look on her face. "I think I ate a squirrel," she said with a grimace as she stuck out her tongue and picked at an imagined piece of fuzz.

Sapphire gagged. "Ugh! That is *sooooo* gross."

"Not to an ogre," Onyx retorted.

"Fine," Topaz snapped. "Next time Amethyst needs to be scared, *you* transform. Look what it did to my blouse!"

"Okay, crew — let's hit the skoots!" Ruby laughed wearily.

Amethyst watched as they rode away in formation into the night. Curling up on her bed next to Wa-wa, she reached for her memory book. "Memory book, on!" she commanded, and the flat screen flashed on to reveal the same old screen saver of her trollementary-school self sticking out her tongue at the camera. "New recording," she said to the book's tiny camera. Suddenly the old picture crackled away to reveal a picture of her fourteen-year-old self sitting on her bed. "That's better," she said.

"What a day," she sighed, pressing a button on the book. "I wonder what's left for tomorrow?"

She and her friends were about to find out.

6

The next afternoon, Amethyst's bright lavender eyes were bathed in the glow of her computer screen as she sat typing at her keyboard. An electronic chime announced an instant troll message from Ruby.

RUBEGrl: What boy do you think is cute?

PINKQT: Do not ever, ever, EVER tell this to anyone ever, alright?

RUBEGrl: Secret's totally safe w/ me!

PINKQT: If I had to absolutely make a choice, I guess I would have to say Coal.

"Coal!" Ruby, Onyx, Sapphire, and Topaz blurted out in unison.

Amethyst jumped about a foot in the air with a startled scream, and Wa-wa barked loudly. Amethyst turned around and got to her feet, only to find her four best friends bent over with laughter.

"Where'd you guys come from?" she asked, still in shock. "Ruby, I thought you were at home. How'd you IM me?"

Ruby waved her spell phone in the air with a troll-tacular grin. "Hey, I got Trollnet access from my spell phone," she giggled, reveling in Amethyst's surprise.

Amethyst smiled. Even though they'd scared the living daylights out of her and Wa-wa, she was always happy to see her buds. Onyx stepped forward and put a hand on Amethyst's shoulder. "Please don't be impressed with Ruby's new toy," she said, rolling her eyes. "C'mon, let's go."

"Where?" Amethyst wondered.

"You'll see," said Ruby with a mischievous grin.

As they stood outside of the Spell Shack at the Trollzopolis mall, Amethyst looked worried.

"Why are we at the Spell Shack?" she asked, staring at the various spell bead displays in the store's window. The Spell Shack was where all of the trollz teens bought their pre-made spell beads. It was a virtual emporium of magic, but it made Amethyst a little nervous. She'd cast only one spell so far — she wasn't exactly an expert.

"To celebrate!" answered Ruby. "You got your glow! You can cast spells! But you need the right spells to cast!"

"We all chipped in a few trollars," added Onyx.

Amethyst's eyes began to well up with gratitude. "I don't know what to say," she said. "I mean, my grandma says spells are a big responsibility, and . . ." She tried to hide her tears by casually wiping her eyes, but her friends nudged one another. Amethyst cried easily. They couldn't count the number of times she'd sobbed at the movies or even while watching nature specials on TV.

"I knew it," Sapphire said, smiling.

"Waterworks," Onyx added. "Every time."

Amethyst gave her friends a sidelong glance and sniffled. "You guys! Nuh-uh!"

"Let's get her inside before she floods the street," Ruby insisted.

Spell beads in assorted shapes and sizes filled the store. They hung from the ceiling and sat behind glass displays like fine jewelry. Amethyst picked up an amber spell bead and inspected it closely. It seemed to glow from within, and its depths appeared to swirl and bubble as if it held great power. It was obviously a very important bead. "What does this one do?" Amethyst asked, holding it up between her thumb and forefinger.

"Causes athlete's foot," Ruby answered, peering at the bead.

"Ick!" Amethyst exclaimed, dropping the trollawful bead in horror. "But it's so pretty."

Her friends gathered around her, happy to share what little spell wisdom they'd learned. "That's the first lesson about buying prefab spells," Sapphire began. "You can't go by the way they look."

Onyx nodded in agreement. "Some of the prettiest ones are also the nastiest," she said. And then glancing at Ruby, she added, "Just like trollz."

Ruby crossed her arms and shot Onyx a frown.

Amethyst was overwhelmed. Looking at all of the spell beads around her, it was nearly impossible to choose. She'd been taught to use her magic sparingly, and this seemed a little indulgent.

"There are certain spells you just have to have," Ruby said, guiding her down the aisle as Sapphire handed her a shopping basket.

"Right," Sapphire agreed. "Like an *overslept late for school bed head emergency* spell."

Was Sapphire ever *late for school?* Amethyst wondered, holding the basket as her friends chose spell beads for her. "I love this one," Ruby declared, holding up another bead. "A *many, many happy returns* spell. It makes your friends forget that they already *gave* you a birthday present."

Onyx held up a glowing blue bead. "Righteous," she said, dropping it into the basket. "A *don't look at me* spell! Makes you invisible to your teacher on those days when you didn't do your homework."

"I never have to use those," Sapphire boasted with her hands on her hips.

"Ooh!" Topaz said. "Here's a *cute boy crush inducer*. Better be careful with this one."

"Ahhh — looking for life's magic," a voice said.

They turned around to find a spellslady who worked at the Spell Shack. The spellslady wore colorful clothes and a mellow smile as she peered at them over her rose-colored granny glasses. "Let me help you find it," she suggested in a hypnotic voice.

Ruby gestured toward Amethyst. "She just got her glow."

"Ah, the sacred awakening," the spellslady said.

"And we'd like to get her a starter set of beads," Ruby added.

"Wise choice," remarked the spellslady, who dramatically held her hand to her forehead and closed her eyes. "Permit me to sense your aura," she said to Amethyst. Suddenly, the spellslady dropped her hand, opened her eyes, and stepped over to a shelf of spell beads. Selecting the appropriate bead, she turned and held it up, incanting:

"A girl with gem just beginning to glow
Needs all the right spells for her magic to flow!"

With that, the spellslady tossed the bead toward Amethyst and it exploded in a cloud of magic dust. Spell beads of all shapes and sizes soon began to fly off the shelves in various parts of the shop along with a string that hovered in midair. The girls watched in astonishment as the various flying beads strung themselves onto the string. Then the string miraculously knotted itself before zipping off toward Amethyst. As Amethyst lifted her left arm, the spell bead bracelet easily slid itself onto her wrist. She looked at it with delight.

"They're the bestest!" she squealed. "Thanks, you guys!"

7

Onyx, Sapphire, Ruby, and Topaz hurriedly handed money to the spellslady and then crowded around Amethyst to get a good look at her new bracelet. Excitedly, they huddled near the shop's entrance, yanking Amethyst's wrist this way and that as they peered at the new beads.

"Which one are you gonna do first?" Sapphire asked, hovering over Amethyst's wrist.

Onyx pushed the girls back as if she were Amethyst's bodyguard. "Back off! Give the girl some room!" she commanded.

Topaz looked sadly at the bracelet. "That bracelet looks so good with her outfit," she said. "It's totally a shame to use it up."

"Topaz," Ruby scolded. "Spells are made to be cast. So what are you waiting for, Amethyst?"

The girls slid into their booth at the food court.

"You've got to try one," Ruby said to Amethyst as she gestured at the spell beads on the bracelet. "And I know on who," she added, surveying the food court.

"*Whom?*" Sapphire asked, correcting Ruby.

"Him," Ruby said, gesturing toward a boy troll who was coming toward them.

"Coal?" asked Amethyst, alarmed.

Coal strolled toward them, walking his skoot. He was the very picture of boy-troll cuteness. But as he glanced over and nodded hello to a friend, he quickly bumped into the trash can, making a loud clanging noise. Wincing in pain, he rubbed his knee, but then accidentally tipped his skoot over and onto his foot. It was like watching a highly choreographed routine of clumsiness.

The girls glanced at Amethyst. She immediately jumped to his defense. "So he's a klutz," she protested. "I still think he's cute!"

"Kind of a shame, though," Ruby said with a sigh. "A guy that semi-hot should at least be semi-cool."

"You really think she's got a spell strong enough to make Coal cool?" Onyx asked. Watching him, it seemed doubtful.

Ruby grabbed Amethyst's wrist and fumbled through her spell beads. Finding one that looked appropriate, she plucked it from the bracelet with ease. "This one ought to do it," she proclaimed.

Suddenly, the girls heard a giant crash. Coal had collided with a table and the table had won. Four angry diners glared at him as he apologetically picked himself up from the wreckage of their meal. This was going to be too tall an order for one troll. "Not enough," Sapphire winced, staring at the small bead in Ruby's hand. "Unless," she added, "we all cast it together."

"Ya think?" Ruby asked.

Sapphire kicked into scientific mode. "Mathematically, it stands to reason," she said with a shrug. "I mean, what's the worst that could happen?"

Amethyst nodded. "I say we do it!"

Ruby motioned for everyone to huddle together. "Get closer, girls!" she ordered. "Everybody touch the bead."

Ruby whispered the spell to her friends.

"OK," Ruby said. "On the count of three. One, two, three!"

**"Though some may say he's just a fool,
Our spell will make that boyfriend cool!"**

8

Boom! The bead vanished and the earth started to shake and tremble. The mall was suddenly wracked with an earthquake! Mall-going trollz screamed as their tables shook and their drinks and food went flying. Trollz ran in every direction, streaming out of stores and heading outside toward safety.

The girls hugged one another for dear life as they watched the trolltastrophe unfold around them. But the quake stopped as quickly as it had begun.

Topaz's eyes bulged in fear. "Did you guys feel that?" she asked, her voice quivering.

"Freaky," Ruby said as she exhaled a huge breath. Then she glanced at her friends' frightened faces. "So, where's Coal?" she laughed. "Did our spell work? Is he cool?"

The girls looked in Coal's direction and their eyes widened in shock. Coal stood in the center of the now deserted food court. He was frozen solid! He wasn't just cool — he had turned to ice! His unfrozen skoot lay on the ground next to him.

"Yeah, I think you could say that," Sapphire stammered in disbelief.

The five trollz surrounded the sparkling, frozen Coal. "Poor Coal!" Amethyst moaned. "Look what we did to him!" She had wanted to make him cool, not a giant ice cube.

But Ruby was impressed. "Wow," she said, surveying their work. "We're more powerful than we thought."

Meanwhile, Topaz was studying Coal intently. "I can see right through him!" she gasped, covering her mouth with her hand. "Somehow that doesn't seem right."

"I don't get it," Sapphire said. "How does he stay frozen in this weather?" She reached her finger out and touched his shoulder, but as she tried to pull her hand away, she realized her finger was stuck. "Uh-oh," she stammered.

On Coal's other side, Onyx was busy trying to talk

him out of his situation. "C'mon, snap out of it!" she barked as she flicked the end of his icy hair. With a snap, small pieces of Coal's hair, now icicles, broke off. Onyx looked guiltily at the haircicle in her hand. "Sorry," she said sheepishly.

Amethyst was completely frizzed out. She grabbed Ruby by the arm and shook her. "What do we do?" she pleaded. "What do we do?"

"Would you chill?" Ruby said. Then she let out a little chuckle. "Hey! Get it? Chill?"

"It's not funny, Ruby!" Amethyst cried, her voice quavering.

"Look, it's gonna wear off!" Ruby assured her friends. "All our spells do! But in the meantime, try not to be so loud. We don't want anyone to notice him."

They glanced over at Sapphire, who was still stuck to him.

"So it would help if you would stop pointing at him!" Ruby added.

Sapphire pulled at her finger, but it didn't budge. "I wish I could," she groaned.

Amethyst grew serious. Spells were nothing to laugh about, no matter how absurd the results. "I'm worried, OK?" she said. "This spell was, like, way bigger than it was supposed to be."

Sensing the truth in what Amethyst had just said, Onyx nodded. "She's right, Ruby," Onyx said. "How many earthquakes have *you* felt during a spell-casting?"

"Maybe the spellslady can help us," Ruby said. "She knows all about spells."

They all nodded in agreement.

"You guys can't just leave us here!" Sapphire pleaded.

"You're right," Onyx replied. "And I've just had an idea." A devilish grin crossed her face.

9

Quickly, the girls hoisted Coal onto his unfrozen skoot, and Sapphire pushed him along — inch by inch — with her finger. The other girls surrounded Coal, providing cover from prying eyes. "I feel like I'm in a parade, and Coal is our float!" Topaz said happily. She had the remarkable ability to have fun and keep a positive outlook even when things were at their absolute bleakest or weirdest.

"There!" Onyx said, pointing to a clothing shop window. A male mannequin stood in the window, clad in a swimsuit, T-shirt, sunglasses, and trucker hat. He was holding a beach ball. Quickly, the girls reached inside the window and removed the mannequin. Sapphire tugged on her finger a few more times and it finally came loose.

"Ow!" she squealed as she shook her burning finger.

They began dressing Coal, the new clothing store mannequin. Topaz picked out Coal's new outfit while Sapphire sucked on her finger. Topaz held a girl's sweater over Coal's frozen chest.

"Isn't this the yummiest?" she asked.

"Topaz!" Ruby reprimanded. "On task!"

"Oh, right!" Topaz mused. "Not his color, anyway," she said as she tossed the sweater aside.

Meanwhile, Onyx wrestled a pair of boxers off a male mannequin that she held tilted over a rack of shirts. The waistband elastic stretched until finally . . . *SNAP!* They came off. Triumphantly, Onyx raised the boxers in the air like a trophy, catching the eye of a teenaged salestroll.

"Excuse me," the salestroll said accusingly as she strided over to Onyx. "Just what do you think you're doing?"

"I'm shopping!" Onyx said, doing her best to sound nonchalant. Suddenly, she remembered that she was holding boxer shorts. The salestroll pursed her lips.

"For my brother," Onyx added, flustered.

Still suspicious, the salestroll peered from behind a clothing rack. She noticed the four other girls huddled by the drapes that concealed the window display. On the other side of the drapes, a mysterious bulge moved around.

"Stop where you are," the salestroll commanded. The girls weren't sure if they should run or answer her. Hands on her hips, the salestroll stormed over to them. "You can't fool me," she said with a scowl. "There's something funny going on here."

The girls looked down guiltily as the salestroll grabbed the edge of the curtain and dramatically yanked it back. In the shop window, Coal was dressed for winter in gloves, a wool cap, a heavy coat, and *boxers*. All of the clothes were way too large and hanging off of him. Under the bizarre display outfit, he still wore a layer of ice over his original clothing. He also had one boot jammed partway onto his foot and a pair of pants draped over his arm. The beach ball that the mannequin had been holding was now tucked under Coal's other arm. Ruby stood in front of him with her chin in her hand as if she were gazing at a statue in a museum.

"What are you doing in there?" the salestroll asked.

Unruffled, Ruby cast a cool glance at the salestroll. "I'm a student at the design school, and I just *love* your totally trollerific display," she replied. The salestroll's suspicions immediately vanished.

"Thank you," she said as the crew quickly backed out of the store. In the shop window, Coal stood in his bizarre new ensemble with the salestroll gazing up at him, delighted.

"We have to get back to the Spell Shack and ask the spellslady what to do!" Amethyst said, a panicked note creeping into her voice.

"Let's go!" Onyx called as the girls broke into a run.

10

When they got to the Spell Shack, they were shocked to find it was closed! Through the glass, they could see that the shop was pitch-black. Ruby rattled the doorknob, but it wouldn't budge.

"Hello?" Amethyst knocked on the door. "Excuse me! Spell emergency!" She pressed her face against the glass of the darkened shop. "We really need your help!" There was no movement inside the shop.

"So what do we do now?" Onyx asked. Suddenly, a breeze whooshed past them. The breeze was so strong that it mussed their hair and knocked them off balance. To the girls' astonishment, the mysterious wind buffeted the door and it slowly creaked open. They stared at the door and exchanged nervous glances.

"But it was locked," Sapphire gasped. "And the lights are out."

Onyx looked into the store and reacted with a start, pointing. "Not all the lights! Look!"

They could see the outline of a door on the far back wall with light escaping around the edges.

"I don't remember a door back there," Ruby shuddered. She was totally spooked.

Onyx rolled her eyes and forced a brave smile. "I bet the spellslady's back there. C'mon!" she said, holding out her hand to Amethyst.

Amethyst gathered her courage and nodded. Taking Onyx's hand, the two eased up to the still mostly closed door. They looked back and the others joined them with trepidation. "Fine," Ruby stammered. "But *I'm* not gonna knock."

Onyx turned to the door. Just as she raised her fist to knock, the door creaked open all by itself. The girls stared at one another, eyes wide with fear. Breathlessly, they steeled themselves and entered.

The back room of the Spell Shack was organic and old-looking, unlike most of the Trollzopolis mall, which tended to be more modern. Shelves and racks looked like they were carved out of elaborate tree roots, and the counter appeared to be a huge mushroom. The shelves were covered with various spell ingredients — jars of dirt, lumps of rock, leaves tied together with string — all of them covered in dust. There didn't appear to be anyone in the back room. The girls entered and looked around.

"I like the retro theme," Topaz said. "But they could use a color consultant."

"Hello," a mysterious voice suddenly droned. The girls' hair stood straight up on end as they let out a petrified scream in unison.

The voice came from a shadowy woman behind the mushroom counter who seemed to have appeared out of nowhere. She smiled at them, unruffled. "I am Obsidian," she said pleasantly. "I have been waiting for you."

The girls looked at one another uneasily. Obsidian was distinctive-looking — a darkly stunning older troll of uncertain age. Her black hair was accented by two white streaks that began at her temples.

"Waiting for us?" Amethyst asked, dumbfounded.

Obsidian smiled. "You were very clever at the clothing store," she said. "I commend you."

Again, the girls were astonished. "How did you know about that?" Ruby asked. Whoever this Obsidian was, she knew more about the girls than *they* did.

"OK, you know a lot of stuff," Amethyst said, looking at Obsidian. "So tell us — do you know why our spell was so powerful?"

"Of course," Obsidian replied. "You used *The Magic of the Five*."

The girls stared at Obsidian and then at one another. What was she talking about?

"How did you know we cast the spell together?" Topaz asked. "And what's *The Magic of the Five*?"

"It is ancient but powerful magic," Obsidian replied. "Few discover it."

"I get it," Ruby mused. "When we work together, we cast a better spell. Cool. So would you please tell Amethyst that it will wear off?"

Obsidian turned her gaze to Amethyst. "Oh, yes. It will definitely wear off," she said.

Amethyst breathed a sigh of relief and smiled. "Oh, great!" she sighed. "So Coal will turn back to normal?"

"Why, no," Obsidian answered. "He will melt."

The girls stared at her, aghast. "But that will ruin his clothes!" Topaz cried.

"And it won't do Coal much good, either," Onyx added wryly.

Obsidian stepped out from behind the counter and held up a hand to calm the girls. They really had no choice but to listen to the wise older troll. "Young ladies," she said calmly. "Do not panic. If you wish to reverse the spell and save your friend, follow me."

Apprehensively, the girls followed Obsidian toward what appeared to be a blank wall. Once again, Obsidian held up her hand, only this time a dark, forbidding doorway opened up in the wall. Mist billowed from it and a deep rush of wind sounds echoed from its depths. Obsidian glanced back at the girls, still wearing her mysterious smile. Then without hesitation, she strode into the darkness of the opening.

The girls were terrified.

"We have to do it," Amethyst shuddered. "For Coal."

11

The girls joined hands and started through the portal with Amethyst in the lead.

The air was so dark and heavy with mist that the trollz struggled to breathe as they made their way through the portal. *What have we gotten ourselves into?* Amethyst wondered. Still holding hands, the girls glanced around nervously at their strange new, misty surroundings.

Topaz grimaced. "Ew!" she said. "It smells like my little brother's room!"

Obsidian stepped out of the mist and stood next to Topaz. "Yes," she said. "The air is thick with the must of the ages."

"See, with him it's dirty sneakers," Topaz countered.

Letting go of her friends' hands, Amethyst approached Obsidian. "What is this place?" she asked. "Why did you bring us here?"

Obsidian raised a hand. "Deep within what you know as the Haunted Woods — *behold* — the ancient world of the trollz!" Obsidian waved her upraised hand, and the mist swirled around them until it finally dispersed, revealing a bizarre landscape.

It was a city, but a city unlike any they'd ever seen. It was a dead city, totally uninhabited, an ancient city that time had forgotten. The stone remnants were so old, they'd decayed and become part of the organic landscape. The land was so barren and rocky that the houses, castles, and shops seemed to be part of the terrain. The ruins stretched to the farthest horizon under the dark, threatening sky.

The girls quickly realized they were very far from Trollzopolis and the modern world. This place was eerie!

"Once, this land was as alive as the great city from which you came," Obsidian said. Then her face grew dark and her eyes narrowed. "But then the dark magic arose and snuffed out the light of life!"

Obsidian looked at the girls. They all appeared scared, except for Onyx. She just rolled her eyes. She'd had just about enough of Obsidian's New Age mumbo jumbo. "Look, lady," Onyx blurted out, "I don't know if you're trying to scare us or what, but would you please stop talking like our drama teacher?"

Obsidian addressed Onyx with a slight smile. "You're a tough one," she remarked.

Onyx shrugged, pleased with herself. "Yeah, I guess so," she mumbled.

"Good. You will have to be," Obsidian warned.

Onyx's cockiness faded away and she listened closely as Obsidian led them across the barren landscape. It was hard to believe anyone had once lived there.

Amethyst shook her mop of pink hair. "I just don't get it!" she asked. "Why are we here? What do all these ruins have to do with us?"

Obsidian spoke matter-of-factly. "You are here because your spell may have awakened the evil that brought this world to an end."

The girls stopped in their tracks. The seriousness of what they'd done dawned even on Topaz. "Even *I* know that's not good," she said.

"Whoa," Sapphire agreed. "And we thought we were in trouble just for turning Coal into a trollcicle."

Amethyst hung her head sadly. She'd only been doing spells a couple of days, and already it seemed she'd brought on the end of the world. If she was growing up, why did she feel like such a foolish trollkin? Obsidian's face softened and she put a comforting hand on Amethyst's shoulder. "Do not despair, child," Obsidian said softly.

Obsidian gestured to the ruined city around them. "When this was the world of the trollz, magic was everywhere. The battle with the dark power so scared your ancestors that they reduced magic to a plaything."

Magic, Obsidian explained, can be a great force — for good as well as for evil. "You and your friends have shown that, together, you can touch some of its deeper powers," she said. "Perhaps you may bring a new era of magic to the trollz. Perhaps this time, they will handle it better."

"Or worse," Onyx added.

Suddenly, another tremor roared underneath them. It was so strong it almost knocked them off their feet. "We must hurry if you want to try to repair what you have done!" Obsidian called to them.

Gelled to the max! Ruby whips off her helmet and shakes out her radically red hair.

Amethyst tells her friends she's got her glow!

Topaz and Sapphire are in awe of Amethyst's magical abilities.

Onyx reveals her plan for getting Amethyst and Ruby to make up.

"Sprig of fir and leaf of clover, turn our Topaz into an ogre!"

Onyx and Sapphire trollin' for spell beads at the Spell Shack.

Ruby shows Amethyst the spell bead that causes athlete's foot!

Oh, no! The trollz' spell is more powerful than they expected.

Topaz is excited to go on a magical adventure.

A stroll through the mall.

Head cheertroll Coral is about to make the first day of school interesting.

Amethyst spots Snarf outside the window.

"HEEEELLLLLP!" the trollz scream to Obsidian.

Uh-oh. Sapphire and her friends are heading to the principal's office.

Amethyst saves a new fave photo in her memory book and labels it...

...Best Friends For Life!

12

The girls eagerly followed Obsidian through the ruins until they came to a grove of trees. A semicircle of massive oaks towered over them, but these weren't normal oak trees — they were all made of gray stone. Despite the fact that a fierce wind blew through the grove, these trees didn't sway. Beneath the trees in the space within the semicircle stood a trollnormous altar carved from a massive tree stump. In the middle of the altar was a brooch in the shape of a four-petaled flower.

"Millennia ago, this oak grove was the most sacred place in the world of the trollz," Obsidian explained. As the girls gaped at the sacred grove, flashes of lightning illuminated the dark, foreboding sky.

"Here resides the greatest of trollz magic," Obsidian continued. "And here, only a true *Uniting of the Five* can have an effect." As if to punctuate her words, another earth tremor rumbled under them. They held on to one another to keep from stumbling as the wind howled wildly around them.

"*Uniting of the Five?*" Amethyst shouted above the wind's wail.

"Is that what we did at the mall?" hollered Ruby.

"Yes!" Obsidian yelled back. "And you must do it again in reverse to undo the spell!"

"Sounds like fun!" Topaz said. Onyx shot her an annoyed look.

"If the fate of the world didn't depend on it!" Topaz added sheepishly.

The wind screeched and another tremor rocked the ground. This one was so strong it sent a crack shooting down the side of the oak altar. Obsidian pointed at the altar and instructed the girls to fit their gems into the altarpiece. "Quickly!" she commanded. "It is the only way!"

The girls fought against the wind, stumbling toward the altar. Once there, they stood in a circle around it and stared, perplexed, at the petals. Onyx reached down and pulled her gemstone from her belly button. The others followed suit, each pulling their gems from their bellies. The petals of the brooch were empty outlines, like settings for jewels, waiting to be filled in. The girls reached their hands down and attempted to insert their gemstones in the settings. Four managed to insert them, but they didn't quite fit. Amethyst stood up, frowning, her gemstone still in her hand.

"They won't fit!" she panicked. "There are only four places! Obsidian, what do we do?" But the girls turned to find that all that was left where Obsidian had been standing was a swirl of dust.

"Obsidian?" Amethyst whispered.

"She's gone!" Sapphire wailed.

Another tremor thundered. The girls heard a massive cracking noise above their heads. They looked up to find that a stone oak had cracked and a large block of stone rained down beside them.

"I can't say I blame her," Ruby chimed in as she surmised their imminent danger.

"She left us here all alone?!" Topaz shrieked.

Suddenly, above the howling wind and trembling ground, they heard the most monstrous growl ever.

"I wouldn't say that," Onyx said, looking at Topaz. They definitely were *not* alone.

"Come on, let's try again!" Amethyst said, staring at the brooch. They snatched their gems out and tried putting them back in different places. They tried forcing two gems into one spot, but still nothing worked. The lightning and wind grew heavier as another oak cracked and sent more stone raining down. Amethyst looked around desperately. "Wait!" she announced suddenly. "I think I've got it!"

She reached in, took Sapphire's gem, and tilted it slightly so that it rested in the petal on a perfect slant. The others reached in and tilted their gems as well. Now the inner facets of each met in the center, forming a place for Amethyst's gem. Very carefully, Amethyst lifted her gem up over the others and prepared to set it down. Suddenly, the strongest tremor yet tore across the ground, cutting a gaping hole in the earth. The tremor threw Amethyst off balance, and her gem went flying from her hand. It bounced off the altar and onto the splitting ground, rolling and bouncing toward the enormous crevasse.

13

"My gem!" Amethyst cried as it bounced across the ground like a tennis ball. Ruby leaped toward it with her arms outstretched. Just as her fingers were about to close around the gem, it slipped from her grasp and teetered on the edge of the crack in the earth. The crack was now large enough to swallow Amethyst whole, but she dove after the gem, anyway. With one final bounce, the gem slipped over the edge. As it started to fall into the crevasse, Amethyst reached in.

"Gotcha!" she cried as she caught the falling gemstone, dangling her body precariously over the edge. Onyx grabbed Amethyst by the legs.

"And I've got you," Onyx said drily.

Ruby then took Onyx by the legs, Sapphire took Ruby, and Topaz held onto Sapphire. Together, they pulled Amethyst back from the crevasse, using all of the strength they could muster. As the girls climbed to their feet and stumbled back to the altar, they heard another hideous growl off in the distance. Sapphire's face went white and she lifted a trembling finger. They followed her frizzed-out stare beyond the stone trees to see a giant, dark creature hunched over and headed their way. It was just a glimpse, but it was all they needed to see.

Amethyst rushed to the altar, holding out her gem. Lowering it to the altarpiece, she pressed it neatly into the flower's center at the intersection of the other four gems.

"There!" she cried, as the gem burst into a glow so bright, it knocked all five girls backward. It was like staring at a star up close.

"You did it, Amethyst!" Topaz cried, throwing her arms around her friend.

"No time for hugs," Sapphire chided as the girls recovered their balance and joined hands. The growl of the monster grew closer.

"Everybody ready?" Ruby asked. "Remember, we have to say it backward. One, two, three!"

Their gems shot a bright, white light into the sky as the wind howled and the great oaks cracked. A tree crashed to the ground with a giant thud as forked lightning flashed over them.

In unison, they chanted:

**"Cool boyfriend that make will spell our,
Fool a just he's say may some though!"**

14

A blinding white flash of light enveloped the girls. When they blinked their eyes open, they found themselves standing in a circle back in the mall. They were silent with disbelief until Topaz spoke.

"See, this is much better!" she said with a sigh.

The others shared her relief until Sapphire stopped suddenly, an alarmed look on her face. "Our gems! We left them in the woods!" she cried. But when she yanked her shirt above her belly button, she saw that her gemstone was back where it belonged. The others did the same and were relieved to find that their gemstones were all back in place, too.

Ruby looked up from her navel, confused. "But this is weird." She frowned. "How'd they get back in there?" As the girls pondered the gemstone mystery, Onyx spotted something else.

"You wanna talk weird, check that out," she said, pointing to the door of the Spell Shack. It was well-lit and *open*. As they looked toward the back, they could clearly see that there was a wall, not a door.

"The Spell Shack's open!" Amethyst said in disbelief.

"And there's no door in the back wall," Sapphire marveled.

"Did all of this even happen?" asked Ruby. "Or am I dreaming it?"

"I hope not," said Topaz. "I have scary-enough dreams on my own without guest-starring in yours!"

"You guys!" Amethyst gasped. "*Coal!*"

As the girls approached the clothing store, they gaped in dismay at the display window where they had left him.

"Oh, no!" Amethyst wailed. "Look!"

Coal was nowhere to be found. The space where he stood was empty, except for a big puddle of water on the floor.

"He melted!" Amethyst cried. "This is terrible! My grandma *warned* me to be careful with magic!" She buried her head in her hands. Suddenly, she heard a familiar voice.

"I mean, what did you think you were doing in that window?"

It was the salestroll, and she was talking to Coal! The irate salestroll stood with her hands on her hips, glaring at a wet, bedraggled, and confused-looking Coal. Apologetically, he handed the wool cap back to her. She was already holding a sopping pile of the clothes he'd been wearing.

"I don't know," he answered sweetly as he added the cap to the pile.

She shot him one last disgusted look. "And don't ever show your face in here again!" she shouted as she stormed back into the store.

"OK," he responded, confused.

Totally mystified, he turned to stumble away when the crew of girls surrounded him.

"Whoa," he said with delight. "Troll babes."

He shot Amethyst a shy smile. "Hi, Amethyst," he said flirtatiously.

"Hi," she said, grinning dreamily from ear to ear.

The others exchanged amused glances as Ruby sidled up to Coal. "Having a rough day?" she asked.

"I have no idea," Coal answered.

"I'll bet you could use a nice cold smoothie," Onyx offered. "Our treat."

"OK," he said with surprise.

As the girls led Coal through the mall toward the food court, Coal suddenly stopped. "Could I maybe have a hot chocolate instead? I don't know why, but I've felt chilled all day."

"One hot chocolate, coming up!" Amethyst said with a giggle.

15

It was Monday morning in Trollzopolis, and a mile-long traffic jam crammed the freeway. A construction worker fought to be heard above the blaring car horns and angry drivers. "I'm thinking yesterday's earthquake caused it," he shouted to his coworker, as he pointed at the gaping hole that had appeared between two lanes.

His coworker shrugged and nonchalantly leaned on his shovel. Suddenly, he heard a monstrous, other-worldly grumbling echoing from within the hole. His eyes bulged as he looked at his friend. A quake then began to shake the highway. Then a blasting roar shot out of the ground, blowing off his helmet and sending his hair into spikes.

"Break time!" the foreman shouted. The men tossed their shovels in the air and ran as another monstrous roar emanated from underneath Trollzopolis.

Across town, Onyx slept soundly in her black and gray bedroom, her dark eyes closed to the world. Suddenly, she bolted upright, her eyes wide with terror. "Wh-wh-wh-whatwasthat?!" she exclaimed, thinking she'd heard the hideous roaring of a monster. But then she noticed her alarm clock was blaring and she relaxed, relieved. *Must've been a nightmare*, she thought.

As Topaz's alarm clock rang, she groggily rolled over, reached her hand out from under the covers, and picked up a fuzzy slipper. "Hello? Hello . . ." she said into the slipper, as if it were a telephone. She awoke with a start and realized she was talking into a slipper. "Huh?" she wondered, scratching her head.

Sapphire's alarm buzzed and she reached over to turn it off. Checking the clock, she gaped at the time. "Oh, no! 7:02? I should've been up by 7:00!" she cried as she leaped out of bed.

In the meantime, Ruby had been out of bed for an hour, raking a comb through her perfect mane of titian hair. *Rube, you are styling*, she thought, giving herself a little wink in the mirror.

In Amethyst's room, a steady stream of clothes was flying out of the closet. Shoes, socks, dresses, and pants all flew through the air as she searched for her favorite

69

anklet. "This is the worst possible thing that could ever possibly happen to me!" she wailed. "Mom! Help!"

Her mother appeared in the doorway to find Amethyst moving around her room like a tornado, opening drawers and tossing clothes in the air.

"I can't find my anklet!" Amethyst shouted, desperate.

"I think Wa-wa found it for you," her mother said, an amused smile on her face.

Amethyst looked down to find Wa-wa tugging on the anklet that she was already wearing.

Amethyst felt a wave of momentary relief, but was once again seized with panic as she realized she couldn't find her purple sweater.

"It's hanging on the back of your closet door," her mother said calmly.

"Oh, right," Amethyst mumbled.

"All you had to do was ask," her mother said warmly.

"Now if I could just find my binder!" Amethyst exclaimed as she rifled through a mound of papers on her desk.

Quietly, her mother stepped into Amethyst's room and picked up the missing binder. "Everything's going to be fine," she said as she handed the binder to Amethyst.

"Mom, it's the first day of high school — in a new school," Amethyst said. "How could that, like, *ever* be fine?"

Her mother sat down on the edge of Amethyst's bed and motioned for Amethyst to join her. "It's the first day for *everyone*," her mother said comfortingly.

"But what if I get lost?" Amethyst said. "What if I can't find my classes? What do I do?"

"All you have to do is ask," her mother answered simply.

Amethyst rolled her eyes and threw up her hands, exasperated. "But, Mom! Ruby says you *always* have to look like you know what you're doing."

She gathered her papers and got to her feet.

"Even if you don't," she added softly.

As Amethyst was getting ready to bolt out the door, her mother stopped her and pulled something from her pocket. "Wait a minute, Amethyst," she said. "I have something for you." She handed Amethyst a necklace with a glowing gem that shone with every color of the rainbow. "It's your grandmother's lucky necklace," she explained. "I know she'll want you to have it."

Great, Amethyst thought, *because I'll need all the luck I can get*. Heartened and grateful, Amethyst gave her mother a quick kiss on the cheek and patted Wa-wa good-bye.

"Well, here I go," Amethyst said to her mom with a shrug and a weak smile.

As Amethyst, Ruby, Sapphire, Onyx, and Topaz skooted toward school, Topaz fretted over her outfit. "Do these shoes go with the skirt?" she worried. "I was going to wear blue ones, but that seemed so obvious."

Sapphire checked out Topaz's shoes and pointed out what she thought was obvious. "Those *are* blue."

"They're not *blue*-blue, they're *bluuuue*," Topaz said with conviction.

"Um, right," Sapphire replied, unconvinced.

"Do shoes really even matter?" Onyx said. She was sporting clunky black boots with magenta straps.

Her four friends stopped and gasped at her in horror. "Of course shoes matter!" they shouted in unison.

"Face it," said Onyx. "We're not going to fit in, anyway."

"That's what worries me, too," Amethyst agreed, nodding her head vigorously.

"*Girlllllls!*" Ruby declared with a confident smirk. "Don't sweat it! You just follow the Rube's lead."

As the girls skooted along, Sapphire checked her watch. "Ohmygosh, we are cutting this so close," she agonized.

"Chill out!" Ruby said as she veered her skoot down a narrow side street. "Shortcut!" The others followed.

Almost an hour later, they found themselves at a dead standstill in the midst of a snarled traffic jam.

Beads of sweat were forming around Sapphire's temples. "Good work," she said, glaring at Ruby. "Now we're officially going to be late."

Amethyst craned her neck for a better look through the dense traffic. It was hard to think straight with the cacophonous noise of the highway all around them. "I think I see a guy from Highway Patrol!" she said hopefully. "Let's ask him when it'll clear up."

But there was no way Ruby was going to ask for help. That would be so uncool. "Puh-*leaze!*" she sighed. She shook her head and skooted off between two stopped cars. "Shortcut number two!" she shouted back to her friends. The others traded looks and skooted after her.

The girls arrived at school looking worse for wear, with leaves and twigs in their hair. *Gee, I'm real glad I spent all that time carefully choosing my outfit,* Topaz thought. As they disembarked from their skoots, they heard the sound of the school bell ringing and ran for the school's entrance.

"Girls!" snapped Ruby. "Hold it!" The girls stopped in their tracks and looked back at Ruby, who sauntered forward with unshakable confidence.

"Troll Stroll," she instructed with a snap of her finger. The others followed, mimicking her distinctive walk. They entered the building troll-strolling like the most styling high-schoolers in Trollzopolis.

17

The girls entered the building confident, cool, and in control. *This isn't so tough*, Amethyst thought. Then, out of nowhere, a cheertroll stepped in front of her.

"Hey! New meat! Where do you think you're going?"

It was Coral, the school's head cheertroll. Behind her stood her cronies, Jade and Opal. They blocked the younger girls' path, their hands on their hips and their chins in the air trollumphantly. They ruled the school and they knew it.

"Um, school?" Topaz answered.

"Not without a late pass!" Coral fumed as she shot the girls a nasty look.

Sapphire glanced at her watch. "I can't believe we're in trouble already!" she said.

The cheertrollz exchanged amused looks. "First, you've

gotta explain why you're late," Coral snorted. She turned to Topaz. "*And* tell me why you think blue goes with that skirt!" she added.

The cheertrollz doubled over with laughter.

"They're not *blue*-blue. They're *bluuuue*," Topaz explained patiently.

Coral rolled her eyes and held up a spell bead. With a nasty look on her face, she chanted:

**"Five dumb newbies, missing classes,
I guess we'll give them all late passes."**

She tossed the spell bead and . . . *poof*! A late pass appeared in each girl's hand.

"Now get to class," Coral commanded. "I assume you know where you're going."

"Actually . . ." Amethyst started, but Ruby interrupted her loudly.

"Sure we do. What do we look like, a bunch of goofs? Come on, girls."

The girls turned to follow Ruby. "We know where we're going?" Topaz asked, delighted.

"Of course not," Ruby answered. "But we can't let *them* know that."

Amethyst looked around at the unfamiliar

surroundings. "Maybe we should ask for help. My mom said . . ."

"Asking is *sooooo* not cool," Ruby cut in. "Knowing is cool. If you act like you know, you're cool. Got it?"

18

As it turned out, knowing wasn't all that easy. The school was like a labyrinth. Each hallway led to three more hallways that looked exactly like the one they'd just been down. "That way," Ruby pointed, feigning confidence. The girls turned down a hallway and came to an intersection that looked exactly like the previous one. In fact, it probably *was* the previous one.

"Ruby, you don't have a clue where we're going, do you?" Onyx groaned.

Sapphire adjusted her glasses and checked her watch for the millionth time that day. "We're so late for our first class that we're early for the second one!" she pronounced wearily.

"Let's ask somebody for help," Amethyst suggested again. She opened the first door she saw and found Coral, Jade, and Opal practicing an inane routine to deafening rock music. Quickly, she closed the door and turned back to her friends. "Uh, maybe not," she whispered.

Ruby removed a spell bead from her necklace. "What we need is a knowledge spell," she said.

"What we need is a map," Sapphire chimed in.

Ignoring her, Ruby concentrated with her eyes shut tight:

"Lost in school on our very first day,
Bring us help to find our way."

She tossed the bead and it erupted in a poof of smoke. As the smoke cleared, the girls waited to see the results of Ruby's spell. They noticed a figure coming toward them through the haze. As he got closer, they were shocked to see that he was an outlandish creature — half goblin, half dog!

As they backed away, the creature stepped closer.

"What is that thing?" asked Amethyst. Her eyes were wide with fear.

"I don't know," Onyx said, scratching her head. "But it doesn't exactly look like help."

"Hello, creature from the smoke," Topaz said guilelessly.

As the goblin dog stepped forward, the girls could see that it was small — about the size of a toy poodle — and not exactly threatening-looking. And its snarl was actually a little smile. It spoke to them in a gruff, deep voice.

"Hey! How ya doin'?" it said. "Snarf's the name. Pleased to meet you!"

As Snarf bounded up to them, Topaz could barely contain herself. "Ohhhhh!" she gushed. "So cuuuuute!"

"But not exactly the kind of help Ruby was looking for," Sapphire observed.

"Go away, puppy!" Onyx commanded.

Snarf cocked his head and looked up at the girls with a puzzled expression. "But I can't go away. You set me free. I'm yours!"

"Yay!" Topaz cheered.

We should have asked for help when we had the chance, Amethyst thought. *Too late now!*

Snarf chased his tail in circles. "So what're we gonna do first? Huh?" he asked, his eyes big and eager.

"As usual, it's up to me to step in and solve the problem," Ruby said with a frown. She leaned in toward the creature and waved her hand. "Shoo!" she commanded.

Snarf's eyes grew big and sad and his mouth turned down into a heartbreaking little frown. It was a pitiful look. And then, in a sudden flash, he transformed into something hideous. His head and teeth ballooned, growing to five times their normal size, and he let out a deep, terrifying growl.

Ruby jumped back in terror, landing in Sapphire's arms. As quickly as Snarf had morphed into a monster, he changed back to his sweet puppy state. Topaz leaned down to pet him, oblivious to what had just happened. "Ruby, are you scared of this sweet little thing?" she asked.

Suddenly, a mysterious teacher appeared at the other end of the hallway. "What's going on here?" he demanded as he approached them.

By the time he reached them, Snarf had disappeared from sight. The teacher was a meek little troll, and he wore clothes that had been in fashion twenty years earlier. The crown of his head was bald, but on either side of his head, bright orange hair rose about three feet in the air. He glared at the girls.

"Well?" he asked menacingly.

"We don't have a dog," Topaz blurted out.

Amethyst elbowed her. The teacher pointed a stern finger at them. "You're supposed to be in class," he scolded. "Where are your hall passes?"

The girls produced their passes and the teacher looked them over.

As he studied the passes, Sapphire turned on the charm. "We're really, really, *really* sorry. We'll never do it again. And I'll bake you some brownies if you won't tell the principal."

The teacher's orange hair seemed to bolt upright in anger. "Dear, I *am* the principal," he said. "And these hall passes are bogus. You'd better come with me."

The girls exchanged miserable glances. Then they turned to follow the principal down the hall.

19

The girls sat in a row inside Principal Trollercrombie's office. "Not the best start for your first day of school, is it, girls?" he asked. "I hope this isn't an indication of . . . of . . . ahhhhh . . . ahhhh . . . achoooooo!" The sneeze was so intense that the principal's hair shot straight out and began to wave. Onyx handed him a tissue from the box on his desk.

"Thank you," he said kindly. "Must be allergy season. I'm allergic to goldenrod and beasts from the realm of darkness."

Amethyst frowned at these words and then glanced down. Something had caught her eye. Topaz's book bag was moving toward Principal Trollercrombie's feet, and a tiny furry tail was sticking out of the bag.

"Sorry, girls," Principal Trollercrombie continued.

"The school rules are that you can get late passes only from the office."

"But how were we supposed to know that?" Sapphire asked.

"You could have asked any teacher," Principal Trollercrombie answered.

The girls shot Ruby pointed looks, which she ignored. Meanwhile, Topaz's book bag was on a rampage. It scooted around the desk and crashed into it, causing the box of tissues to fall to the floor.

Principal Trollercrombie's eyes watered as he spoke. "It's Coral and her crew playing tricks on the new kids again," he wheezed. "I'll take care of them. And since it's your first day, I'll cut you a break. No punishment this time, but I'd better not catch you breaking any more rules. Here are some school maps to help you get around. Now get to Mr. Trollheimer's class!" He reached for the tissues, but the box was gone. He shrugged his shoulders and blew his nose on one of the phony late passes.

Topaz managed to grab her book bag as it scooted by her. As the girls hurried out of the office, Principal Trollercrombie almost blew down the door with another sneeze.

Once they were back in the hallway, Snarf wriggled out of the bag. "You weren't going to keep me in there forever, were you?" he asked.

"I wouldn't have minded," Ruby muttered under her breath.

"You have to stay out of sight or we'll be in big trouble," Amethyst warned him.

As the girls deliberated over what to do with him, Topaz picked him up protectively.

"I'll take care of him," she said, snuggling him. Then she glanced into her book bag and groaned. "Ew! Somebody needs to be book bag trained!"

Topaz opened the nearest exit door and placed Snarf outside behind a cluster of bushes. "You'll have to wait here until the end of the day," she told him. "But I promise I'll come back for you."

The girls walked into homeroom and handed Mr. Trollheimer their real hall passes. Amethyst took a seat and pulled out a book. Outside the window, Snarf bounced up and down, whimpering and whining. He caught Amethyst's eye, and she shooed him away, but he continued to bounce around. Amethyst nudged Topaz and motioned to the window. The two girls watched in horror as Snarf squeezed himself in under the shut window.

His whole body compressed itself flat to slip through the crack, and then he re-inflated on the inside with a small *pop*!

"Neat trick, huh?" he asked, smiling proudly at the panic-stricken girls. Amethyst quickly grabbed Snarf and threw him into Sapphire's hair, where he disappeared under her mane of blue locks. Sapphire looked up from her book. Amethyst gestured wildly at her to indicate that Snarf was hiding out in her hair.

"Stay put!" Amethyst hissed at Snarf through the hair.

Mr. Trollheimer looked up from his desk with a frown.

"OK, who's talking?" he asked.

Amethyst did her best to feign interest in her book. Sapphire, on the other hand, was actually able to go back to her book. As Sapphire's hairdo moved about wildly, Mr. Trollheimer appeared at Amethyst's side.

"Is everything OK over here?" he asked with a raised eyebrow. "It's Amethyst, right?"

"Oh! Yes, sir. Everything's gellin'!" she answered innocently.

"Gellin', huh?" Mr. Trollheimer asked curiously. "That's a good thing, right?"

"Yes, sir, Mr. Trollheimer, sir!" Amethyst answered brightly, sitting up in her chair.

Mr. Trollheimer suddenly noticed Amethyst's necklace. "And, um, where did you get that lovely necklace?" he asked.

"It's from my grandmother," Amethyst answered sweetly.

All of a sudden, Snarf began grumbling audibly. Amethyst and Mr. Trollheimer both turned to Sapphire.

Sapphire looked up with wide, innocent eyes. "Must be my stomach," she said with a sigh. "I missed breakfast."

Mr. Trollheimer raised an eyebrow and opened his mouth to respond, but the ringing bell cut him off.

20

"Saved by the bell!" Amethyst cried happily as she jumped up from her desk and followed the others out the door. The girls hurried down the hall and hastily ducked into a corner. "You've got something in your hair," Topaz told Sapphire drily, pulling Snarf out of her do.

"Um, yeah," said Sapphire. "I kind of figured that out."

Topaz stuffed Snarf into her book bag, and the girls wandered outside. Flint was perched on a bench, playing his guitar for an adoring audience of high school girls.

"At least Flint's having a good day," Amethyst said with a sigh.

"I'll bet everybody is but us!" Topaz moaned as Coal approached the group. "Hey, Amethyst!" Coal said. "How are ya do —" he suddenly ran headfirst into a planter.

"Well, almost everybody," Onyx said wryly.

The girls headed toward the deserted bleachers near the ball field. No one seemed to be around, so Topaz removed Snarf from her book bag.

"How are you doing, little fella?" she asked.

"What are we gonna do with this thing?" Amethyst moaned.

Snarf was suddenly offended. "Thing?" he protested. "I ain't no thing! I'm a Snarf! And I've got big plans for us!"

"You guys deal with this, OK?" Ruby said, annoyed. "It's not my problem, and it's totally ruining my first day."

"Excuse me?" Onyx snapped back. "If you'd let us ask for help when we first got to school, none of this would have happened!"

Amethyst stood between them. "Calm down," she said soothingly. "We'll think of something and everything will be fine. . . ." She trailed off, noticing Coral and her cronies approaching. "Or not," she added with a sigh.

"Yo! New meat!" Coral hollered at them. Topaz stuffed Snarf back in the bag.

"We just got chewed out 'cause you squealed about the late passes," Coral snarled.

"We didn't squeal on anybody," Onyx snapped back.

"We even got detention," Coral said, ignoring Onyx. "Thanks to you trollz!"

"We're sorry?" Amethyst offered.

"You bet you're gonna be," Coral threatened. "Just wait and see."

21

The three cheertrollz advanced on the girls. Suddenly Snarf leaped from the book bag. Baring his fangs, he grew to at least twice his normal size.

The cheertrollz screamed and recoiled as Amethyst grabbed Snarf and pulled him back inside the bag, his snapping fangs mere inches from Coral.

"Wh-wh-what is that thing?" Coral stammered, horrified.

"We're not really sure," Topaz answered. "But isn't he *cute*?"

At this, Snarf leaped from the bag again, growing even larger than before. "*Rorrowwwwrrrr!*" he growled menacingly. The cheertrollz screamed and ran.

As the cheertrollz disappeared, Snarf shrank, calmed down, and smiled a satisfied little grin.

"Pssst," Onyx whispered, motioning her friends to come closer. "Trollz, over here."

The girls huddled nearby, away from Snarf. "What is it, Onyx?" Sapphire asked. "You look like you saw a ghost."

Onyx checked to make sure Snarf wasn't listening. "I just realized where I heard that sound before," she whispered. "In the oak grove in the ancient world!"

The girls gasped in unison and glanced at Snarf.

"Snarf's that creepy creature we saw down there?" Sapphire asked.

"It can't be," Amethyst said in disbelief.

"Sure it can!" Snarf shouted. He had suddenly appeared right there beside them, flashing a toothy grin. The startled girls stepped back.

"Yeah, I've been trapped down there for centuries, but you girls set me free!" Snarf said happily. "And now you've gotta help me free my master!"

The girls stepped farther back, terrified.

"Your m-m-master?" Sapphire stuttered.

"C'mon, please?" Snarf begged. "I'll be your best friend forever! It'll just take a second. Whaddya say?"

The five girls shook their heads.

"Uh, sorry," Sapphire said. "We'd, uh, love to, but we've gotta get to math class."

As the trollz tried to walk past him, Snarf suddenly grew very angry and ballooned to three times his normal size.

"No!" he barked nastily as he blocked their path.

The girls grasped one another, terrified. In the next moment, though, Snarf shrank back to his original size.

Suddenly, Onyx had an idea. She grabbed a stick and heaved it across the field. "Hey, Snarf," she shouted. "Fetch!"

Instinctively, Snarf began to chase the stick, but then he stopped in his tracks and turned. "You're not trying to ditch me, are ya?" he snarled in a menacing voice. "You *are* going to help my master, right?"

"Wrong!" Ruby shouted. She was tired of being pushed around by this evil little puppy dog. "Whoever this master is, we don't care. We've got things to do. So SCRAM! GET OUTTA MY FACE! GOT IT!?"

The other girls turned to Ruby, suddenly fearful. What had she done?

Snarf began to whimper.

Topaz hurried to his side. "Awwww," she soothed. "Look what you did, Ruby."

Snarf continued to sniffle, turning away from them. And then, in a terrifying instant, he grew eight feet tall and sprouted glistening fangs!

"You're against me!" he roared.

The girls' hair stood straight up in terror as they let out a massive collective scream. They turned and ran, screaming as they fled.

As Snarf tore after the girls, other students noticed the beast and ran from it, yelling for their lives. But Flint was so lost in his soulful guitar playing that he didn't even notice the madcap chase going on around him.

From a classroom window, Mr. Trollheimer took in the chaotic scene. "Oh, no," he said. "It's Snarf!" He picked up the nearest phone and quickly dialed.

22

The girls raced back into the building in an attempt to get away. They headed down one hallway and up another, but there was no escaping Snarf.

"Uh-oh!" Onyx called out. The hallway came to a dead end at a set of double doors that was locked with a combination lock and chains. Snarf was closing in on them. Sapphire pulled out a spell bead.

"Girls, I think it's time for a little more magic," she said. She closed her eyes, held up the spell bead, and began a chant:

> "Let the doors open wide,
> Let the lock not defeat us,
> 'Cause there's a mean doggie coming,
> And he's going to eat us!"

She tossed the spell bead at the double doors, and it exploded in a cloud of smoke. Through the smoke, the girls could see the combination lock open and the chain unwrap itself as they both floated away.

Amethyst opened the door quickly and the others raced in. They closed the doors behind them and turned to see that they were now trapped in the school's massive gymnasium.

"Follow me!" Ruby hollered.

"Isn't that how we got here in the first place?" Amethyst snapped.

But Snarf crashed through the gymnasium's double doors, and the girls had no time to question Ruby's judgment. With one swipe of his claw, Snarf managed to roll a whole set of bleachers in front of the doors behind him, blockading them inside the gym.

The girls followed Ruby as she hopped up to the gym's climbing ropes and began to swing from one rope to the next. Finally, she bounced off a trampoline and flew to the other side of the gym. The other girls quickly followed, but Snarf was too fast for them. He closed in on them with his teeth bared. They were now genuinely trapped.

"See what happens when you use magic you don't understand?" he hissed, slobber dripping from his mouth.

"W-we didn't mean to," Ruby stammered.

"What if we promise not to do it again?" Amethyst begged.

"Too late!" Snarf growled.

Suddenly, a loud blast exploded behind the bleachers. As the smoke cleared, Mr. Trollheimer and Obsidian dashed into the gym.

"Obsidian!" Topaz exclaimed. "How'd she do that?"

"Do we really care?" Onyx said wryly.

"Can we ask for help now?" Amethyst asked, glaring at Ruby.

"After all that's happened, I'd have to say . . . YES!" Ruby shouted. She turned toward the two adults. "HEEEELLLLP!" she screamed at the top of her lungs.

As Mr. Trollheimer and Obsidian tried to reach the girls, Snarf turned on them, growing to at least twenty trollnormous feet tall.

"Amethyst!" Obsidian called. "Use a spell from your necklace. It's our only hope!"

Amethyst grasped her necklace, and the other girls followed, each putting a hand on the gem and scrunching their eyes closed in concentration. The rainbow colors began to glow and pulse with power as Amethyst chanted:

"What we Pive Priends couldn't do alone,
We'll do together, Por together we've grown,
With help Prom magic still unknown,
Magic Prom the heart of this sacred stone!"

The whole gymnasium began to rock and rattle as the rainbow of colors spilled from the gem, floating through the space with intensity. Snarf watched the colors pulse and glow as they swirled and danced around him.

"Hey, where'd you get that thing?" he asked, panicking. "You're not supposed to have that! Somebody might get hurt! Somebody might —"

Snarf's words drifted off as he abruptly vanished with a brilliant flash. The pulsating colors slowly dissipated and vanished like a fog.

The girls ran to Obsidian and Mr. Trollheimer, still shaken.

"Thanks!" Amethyst smiled. "We couldn't have done that without your help."

"All you had to do was ask," Mr. Trollheimer said kindly.

Onyx turned to Obsidian and raised an eyebrow. "What are you doing here, anyway?" she asked.

"Mr. Trollheimer called me," she answered slyly.

"You two know each other?" Amethyst asked, amazed. This new school year was certainly going to be interesting.

"We go way back," Mr. Trollheimer answered casually.

"Not bad," Obsidian said, surveying the scene. "You girls are learning,"

"Not bad?!" Ruby protested. "Did you *see* that thing go POOF?! We rule!"

Obsidian shook her head. "He may have only run away," she warned. "It isn't easy to get rid of a beast like that."

"Who is the master he talked about?" Amethyst asked.

"Let's not worry about him for now," Obsidian said, glancing over at Mr. Trollheimer with a concerned look on her face.

"For now, let's go see how we can explain all this to the principal," Mr. Trollheimer said.

The girls slumped as Mr. Trollheimer gestured toward the door.

23

At home, Amethyst dropped her books and flopped down on her bed. Wa-wa curled up next to her, excitedly licking her face. She scratched his head as she opened her memory book. "Memory book, on!" she commanded. "I want to view the last three days!" she said eagerly. The memory book's screen dissolved to reveal Amethyst and Ruby sharing a banana split as Sapphire slurped a milkshake and waved to the camera. The camera then zoomed back to reveal Topaz as an ogre, fussing over her hair.

"Ooh! Onyx! No!" Topaz cried. "My hair's a mess!" She waved her hands in front of the lens.

Laughing, Amethyst scratched Wa-wa behind his ears. "I'm so glad I still fit in with my friends, Wa-wa," she sighed, as the memory book cut to Coal posing in the clothing store window, striking a goofy pose.

"We have so much fun when we're together," she said, thinking of their many trials and trollulations. "But it's more than that. When we're together, we can do things other trollz can't. It's kinda scary." Wa-wa let out a big yawn. "But I guess you're not interested in that," she said, patting his head.

Staring back at her memory book, she watched as Onyx, Topaz, Sapphire, and she walked toward the camera. "Wait, guys!" Ruby yelled from off camera. "Hold it right there!" Ruby set the camera down and ran into the shot, joining her friends.

"Troll Stroll!" she declared as the five girls ambled toward the camera in unison. As they neared the camera, Topaz accidentally kicked it, knocking it over. The memory book cut to black while the girls doubled over with laughter.

"Oops! My bad!" Topaz laughed, grabbing the camera and propping it up.

Amethyst smiled and clicked a button on the keyboard. "I think I'll rename this file," she said.

Then she typed the new name: **Best Friends For Life.**

Congratrollations!

You get 50 Trollars to spend on Trollz.com
just for buying this book! After you've read
the book go to Trollz.com and type in
the code below to collect your 50 Trollars
and have a chance to earn 300 more!

0-439-73387-1nr4430g49tt5

Big Hair, Wild Spells, Cool Music!

Enter the magical world of *Trollz* on DVD.

Coming to DVD September 2005!

New full-length never-before-seen movies.

Comes with great extra stuff including *Trollz* memory book & music videos!

Available at a retailer near you.

www.trollz.com.